For Angelina June, with love

Special thanks to Valerie Wilding

ORCHARD BOOKS

First published in Great Britain in 2016 by The Watts Publishing Group

1 3 5 7 9 10 8 6 4 2

Text copyright © Working Partners Ltd 2016
Illustrations copyright © Working Partners Ltd 2016
Series created by Working Partners Ltd

A CIP catalogue record for this book is available from the British Library.

ISBN 978 1 40834 119 3

Printed in Great Britain

The paper and board used in this book are made from wood from responsible sources

Orchard Books
An imprint of Hachette Children's Group
Part of The Watts Publishing Group Limited
Carmelite House, 50 Victoria Embankment, London EC4Y 0DZ

An Hachette UK Company
www.hachette.co.uk
www.hachettechildrens.co.uk

Millie Picklesnout's Wild Ride

Daisy Meadows

ORCHARD

To Friendship
Forest

Shimmer Lake

Snowy Swimming School

Snowy
Swimmin

Beach

Pier

Can you keep a secret? I thought you could!

Then I'll tell you about an enchanted wood.

It lies through the door in the old oak tree,

Let's go there now - just follow me!

We'll find adventure that never ends,

And meet the Magic Animal Friends!

Love,
Goldie the Cat

Contents

CHAPTER ONE

A Golden Visitor

"Let's fill it up!" said Lily Hart. She aimed the hose towards the big hole that was going to be a new pond.

Lily and her best friend, Jess Forester, were in the Harts' garden. Nearby was the Helping Paw Wildlife Hospital, which Lily's parents ran in a barn behind

their cottage. The new pond was for the

poorly ducklings who were staying there.

The girls were sure that other creatures

would use it, too – goslings, frogs,

dragonflies and newts. All were welcome!

Lily held the hose ready as Jess

crunched through crisp autumn

leaves to turn on the garden

tap. Water spurted out of

the end of the hose and

started to fill the pond.

"Quack! Quack! Quack!"

Three fluffy yellow ducklings waddled towards the pond. Lily wiggled the hose, splashing them a little. They quacked and flapped, enjoying their shower in the warm sunshine!

"Our first visitors!" said Jess with a laugh, as she hurried back to Lily.

Lily lay down the hose so it dangled over the pond's edge. "It'll take ages to fill," she said. "Why don't we—Listen! Did you hear that?"

A soft mew came from behind them.

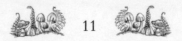 11

The girls spun around to see a beautiful green-eyed cat. Her golden fur gleamed in the sunshine.

"Goldie!" cried Jess. "It's wonderful to see you again!"

Goldie was their special friend. She came from Friendship Forest – a secret, magical world where all the animals could talk! They lived in cosy dens and cottages, and loved chatting over honey milkshakes in the Toadstool Café. Goldie often took Jess and Lily there to visit their animal friends, and they'd shared many adventures.

The girls stroked the purring cat.

"She's come to take us to Friendship Forest!" said Lily, her eyes shining.

Jess grinned, but then she looked serious. "I just hope Grizelda isn't up to her old tricks," she said.

Grizelda was a horrible witch who wanted to drive all the animals away from the forest, so she could have it all to herself.

"We'll soon find out," said Lily. "Let's follow Goldie!"

The cat was running towards Brightley Stream at the bottom of the garden, her

13

fur glinting in the autumn sunshine. Lily
and Jess hurried after her. They jumped
across the stream's stepping stones into
Brightley Meadow, and headed towards a
dead-looking tree.

Jess and Lily watched in delight as it
burst into life, sprouting yellow, red and
orange leaves that were so bright they
seemed to glow. A flock of goldfinches
swooped down to feast on thistle seeds
in the grass below, while a squirrel raced
around the branches, gathering acorns for
his winter store.

Goldie patted the tree with her paw,

and the girls bent to
read the two words
that appeared in
the bark.

"Friendship
Forest!"

A small door
appeared in the

trunk. With an excited glance at Lily, Jess
turned its leaf-shaped handle.

Shimmering light shone out and they
followed Goldie inside. The girls held
hands and felt the familiar tingle that
meant they were shrinking a little.

When the golden glow faded, they
found themselves in a sun-dappled forest
glade. The air was warm, and sweet with
the scent of honeyberry flowers.

And there stood Goldie, almost as tall
as the girls, and wearing her glittery scarf.

She smiled and hugged them.
"Welcome to Friendship Forest!"

"It's great to be back!" said Lily.

Jess held Goldie's paw. "Is Grizelda
causing trouble?"

"No, we haven't seen her," said Goldie.
"I've brought you here for some fun!"

Lily felt a tingle of excitement. "I can't

wait! Where are we going?"

Goldie smiled. "To the Friendship Forest Funfair! Come on!"

"Hooray!" said Jess, as they hurried past little cottages tucked among tree roots or nestled on branches. "We love fairs. Where is it?"

"Across Shimmer Lake," Goldie explained. "On Sapphire Isle!"

"Great!" said Lily. "We'll see some of our friends again!"

After a lovely walk through the forest, they reached Shimmer Lake. A beautiful sailing boat was waiting at the water's

edge. On deck, waving like mad, was a little beaver and her dad.

"Phoebe Paddlefoot!" cried Jess.

Mr Paddlefoot put out a paw to help them up the gangplank. "Welcome aboard!"

Phoebe hugged the girls.

"It's lovely to see you," said Lily. "Are you taking us across the lake?"

"Yes," said Phoebe. "We're going to have so much fun today!"

Lily and Jess hoped so, but they couldn't help remembering their last couple of visits to the island. Grizelda had stolen two of the magical sapphires that protected it. She wanted the island for her holiday home, and she knew that if she ruined the lake, the animals would have to leave. So far, Grizelda had stolen the sapphire guarded by Katie Prettywhiskers's family, which kept the lake at the right temperature, and the one guarded by the Paddlefoots, which kept the lake clean. But Goldie and the girls had got the sapphires back, and they were now in very safe places.

"I hope Grizelda doesn't try to steal another sapphire today," Jess whispered.

 20

"If she does, we'll be ready to get it back," Lily replied.

As they drew near the island, a long wooden pier came into view.

"There's the funfair!" cried Jess, pointing to a tall helter-skelter, towering over a giant water slide.

The pier was decorated with balloons and colourful streamers. The air was filled

with laughter, squeals and jingle-jangle
music.

It looked so exciting that all the girls'
worries about Grizelda disappeared!

 22

CHAPTER TWO

The Water Whirl

There were rides and stalls all along the pier. The girls saw bumper carts, a teacup ride and a boat swinging back and forth.

As they queued to get in, they spotted Lottie Littlestripe the badger whizzing round and round the helter-skelter. The Woollyhop lambs and the Greenhop

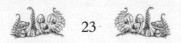

frogs sprang up and down on a bouncy

castle, while a young hedgehog watched

enviously.

"Emily Prickleback can't go on the

bouncy castle because her prickles would

burst it," said Phoebe.

"Poor Emily," said Jess. "But there are

lots of other things she can do!"

At the ticket booth, they met a little

pink piglet with the curliest tail they'd

ever seen. She wore a big smile and a

pretty gold necklace.

"Hello, Goldie!" she said. "And you

must be Jess and Lily!"

"That's right!" Jess said, with a grin.

"I'm Millie Picklesnout! My family runs the funfair," said the piglet. "I'll show you around! You don't need tickets, because you saved those two sapphires from horrible Grizelda. You're our special guests!"

"Thanks, Millie!" said Lily.

"Your funfair looks great!" added Jess.

Millie smiled. "It's the best ever!"

They passed a popcorn machine called
the Nonstop Pop'n'Tops.

Jess grinned. "I bet Mr Cleverfeather the
owl invented that!"

"He did," said Millie. "It pops out
twenty different flavours at the touch of a
button. And it never runs out!"

Choo-choo!

The girls jumped clear of the Tiny
Train for Teeny Tots. Its passengers
were the Twinkletail mice and the
Nibblesqueak hamsters. They squeaked

with delight and waved to the girls.

"Here's the Hall of Funny Mirrors," said Millie, pulling a bead curtain aside.

They peeped in and Jess saw her reflection in a tall mirror.

Everyone giggled. She had a head the size of an orange, a long thin neck and enormous feet!

Millie's little pink snout wrinkled with laughter. She put her tiny trotters into the girls' hands. "Come and see my favourite ride!"

They went to the edge of the pier. Hovering above the lake was a merry-go-round, with carved wooden seahorses in different colours. The seahorses all stood around a tall pillar that rose out of the water.

"Wow! Those seahorses are floating in the air," Lily said in amazement.

Millie smiled proudly. "It's the Water Whirl!"

Squeak! Squeak!

Another little piglet ran over. He wore blue shorts with yellow braces and had a tuft of white bristles between his ears.

"That's my brother, Benji," said Millie.

The piglet squealed with excitement. "You're those girls who helped save the forest from that horrid witch! You're brave!"

"They're going to try the Water Whirl," said Millie.

"Jess and Lily, take your shoes and socks off."

When that was done, Millie called, "Ready, Dad!"

A tall pig wearing a green waistcoat pulled a long lever and the seahorses bobbed slowly in a circle around the pillar.

"Get ready to climb on!" called Mr Picklesnout.

As the first seahorse reached the pier,
Benji scrambled onto it. Lily was next,
feeling rather nervous. Then Goldie
mounted her seahorse, followed by Jess
and Millie.

Lily noticed that her seahorse had a
pale blue shell on its forehead. Jess's had a
yellow one.

"Here we go!" said Millie.

Clickety-clackety music played as they

gathered speed. The seahorses bobbed up, then down, so the riders' feet dipped into the water.

"This is amazing!" Jess cried, as they circled swiftly around.

Millie laughed. "It's the most exciting ride in the funfair!"

Eventually, the ride slowed to a halt.

Lily drew a deep breath. "That was brilliant!"

Jess was looking at the pillar in the middle, which was covered in carved flowers. "It's so pretty," she said.

"It is," said Millie, "and it's got a secret

 32

inside." She looked around to check no one else was nearby. "One of the magical sapphires is hidden inside it," she whispered. "It keeps the lake calm. Our family guards it."

She touched a silver shell on her seahorse's forehead and it bobbed towards the pillar. "Let me show you," Millie called. "Touch your shells, and your seahorses will follow!"

Jess, Lily, Goldie and Benji did as she said. Their seahorses floated gently up and down as they followed the little piglet. It felt like flying!

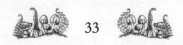

33

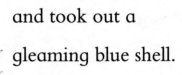
Millie glanced around again to make
sure no one was looking, then she tapped
a waterlily carving on the pillar. A hidden
door sprang open. Millie reached inside
and took out a
gleaming blue shell.

The girls held their
breath.

Millie opened
the shell. Inside was
a dazzling blue
sapphire, shaped like
a flower.

"What a brilliant hiding place," said

 34

Jess. "Even Grizelda's magic couldn't find it there!"

Millie took the sapphire from its shell. "Have a closer look," she said, handing it to Lily.

The girls watched it flash and sparkle in the sunlight.

"It's so beautiful," said Lily.

"It's like gazing into the deep blue sea," said Jess. "But you'd better put it back before anything happens to it."

"Yes," said Millie, taking it from her. "As long as the sapphire's in its shell, it's safe."

But before she could replace the

35

sapphire, the Water Whirl lurched off again – far too quickly. The girls clutched on to their seahorses' necks so they wouldn't fall off.

"Hey!" cried Benji. "What's happening?"

"I don't know!" Millie cried as they bobbed about.

Lily gasped. "Look!"

A slimy, seaweed-covered steamboat was heading for the pier. Stinky sparks spurted from its funnel, which blew a loud, screechy blast.

A tall thin woman, with green hair

 36

whipping around her face, steered the
boat straight for the Water Whirl. Her
hands were waving in the air, shooting
out black sparks.

"So that's why the ride's going so fast!"
Jess cried. "Grizelda's horrible magic!"

CHAPTER THREE

Shimmer Lake Goes Wild

The witch swirled her black cloak over her purple tunic. She shrieked with laughter as the girls and the Picklesnouts clung on to their speeding seahorses. "Hold on tight!" she cackled. "Or you'll fall into the water! Ha!"

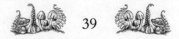

"Make the ride slow down, Grizelda," called Goldie. "It's dangerous!"

Grizelda shook her head. "If you're busy holding on, you won't be able to stop my wonderful new plan!"

Millie gasped. "She must be after the sapphire," she whispered to Lily. She held it behind her back, her curly tail shaking with worry.

Three small, blue creatures jumped out from behind Grizelda and stood in a row on the deck.

"The water imps!" Jess gasped, as her seahorse spun her around.

Jess and Lily had met the water imps on their last adventures on Sapphire Isle. They wore tatty trousers and stripy tops, like scruffy little pirates. The girls recognised Kelp with his wooden leg and seaweed fishing net. Shrimp wore his arm bands, and Urchin was stuffing a grubby sandwich into her mouth.

"There are usually four imps," Lily said. She looked around, holding tightly to her seahorse. "Where's Barnacle?"

Grizelda screeched with laughter. "Silly creatures!" she cackled. "Barnacle's been spying on you, waiting for you to take the sapphire out of its shell."

One of the seahorse's tails twitched, and Barnacle popped out from underneath it. She rubbed her sticky hands in glee, then leapt onto Millie's seahorse.

The piglet shrieked as Barnacle reached for the sapphire. "No!" she cried.

Lily and Jess tried to stretch across to

help Millie, but
it was no good
– their seahorses
were spinning so

fast that it was all they could do to hold on.

Barnacle grabbed the sapphire with
her sticky fingers. "Catch, me hearties!"
she yelled to the other three imps. They
leaped off Grizelda's boat and swam
through the water. Barnacle threw the
sapphire towards them and Kelp caught it
in his net.

Instantly, the lake's surface grew
choppy. Water slapped the pier, splashing

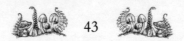

the animals standing on it. They all squeaked and squawked in fright. Huge waves rolled across the lake, battering the seahorses. The girls clung on tightly, their wet hair sticking to their faces.

From the pier came an angry snort. Then Mr Picklesnout's voice shouted, "Hold on!" He pushed the lever to stop the Water Whirl.

As it slowed, he pulled the friends to safety – first Millie, then

Goldie and Lily. Jess leapt off by herself,
so Mr Picklesnout reached for Benji.

But, just then, a giant wave hit Benji's
seahorse. He tumbled off and fell into the
churning water.

Goldie and the girls stared in horror.

On her steamboat, Grizelda was
cackling with delight. "These crashing
waves will sweep you animals away!" she
cried. "Just like that little piggy!"

"Help!" squeaked

Benji.

Millie squealed,

and leaped in

after him. "I'll save you!" she cried, grabbing his trotter. The girls reached out for her and, between them, they pulled the piglets to safety.

Jess lifted Benji into Mr Picklesnout's arms, while Lily cuddled Millie. "You're the bravest little piglet ever," she told her.

But Millie's tail drooped sadly. "They took the sapphire," she said. Then she glared at Grizelda. "We'll get it back, you horrible witch!"

"My imps will make sure you don't," said Grizelda. She pointed a bony finger, shooting sparks at a red wooden seahorse.

It bobbed away from the Water Whirl.

"Climb on!" she yelled to the water imps.

Goldie and the girls stared in dismay as the imps rode the red seahorse across the wild water, carrying the sapphire with them.

"You'll never get it back now!" Grizelda crowed. "Sapphire Isle will soon be mine!" She spun

the steering wheel and the boat turned
and steamed away.

Waves broke over the pier, soaking the
shivering animals and drenching the rides.

"Find shelter, everyone!" Mr
Picklesnout shouted over the water's
crashing and splashing.

Lily and Jess grabbed their shoes and
socks, hopping along in their rush to put
them on and escape the wild water at the
same time. The animals scurried away
from the shore, heading for safety.

The girls, Goldie and the Picklesnouts
scrambled up a hillside, then paused to

catch their breath.

"We'll get the sapphire back and fix this," panted Lily. "We promise."

Mr Picklesnout wrung the water out of his tail. "But where have the imps taken it?" he wondered sadly.

"We'll find out," said Jess. "I know! Admiral Greatwing the albatross has a magical map – it shows where all the sapphires are. We'll go and borrow it."

Millie turned to Mr Picklesnout. "Dad, I can go, can't I? I know the way to Admiral Greatwing's house, and I'll protect the girls from danger. and it'll be an adventure—"

"Whoa! Slow down!" smiled her dad.
"Yes, you can go. You're a very brave
piglet."

"We'll look after her," promised Lily.

And off they went, following Millie
along a gravel path.

"I just hope we can find the sapphire
this time," Jess whispered to Lily. "The imps
could have taken it anywhere by now."

Lily nodded. "But we've done it before
and we can do it again! We'll have to –
or Grizelda will take control of Sapphire
Isle… and all of Friendship Forest!"

CHAPTER FOUR

Brightbeaks in Danger

Admiral Greatwing the albatross lived in an old ship perched on top of a hill. When the friends arrived, he was in his crow's nest, which was a big barrel fixed to a tall pole. His sailor's hat was tipped back as he gazed through his telescope.

"Hello!" Jess shouted.

 51

"By my feathers!" he boomed. "Goldie and the girls! And is that little Millie Picklesnout?"

"Yes!" said the piglet. "And we need your help!"

The admiral spread his enormous wings and glided to the ground. "Come inside," he said.

The room they entered was filled with furniture, old maps, ships' bells and wooden chests.

"I was watching the lake through my telescope," the admiral nodded. "Haven't seen waves like that since I sailed single-winged across the Sea of Storms. How can I help?"

Jess explained about Grizelda's imps stealing the sapphire.

"I'll get my map," said the admiral. He unlocked a chest with a brass key, lifted the lid and burrowed inside.

"Found it!" he boomed. He unrolled the map, and everyone crowded around.

It showed Sapphire Isle, with names of villages, rivers and coves written on it. Four blue symbols showed where the sapphires were. The girls knew that if a sapphire moved, so did its symbol.

Goldie pointed her paw to one of the sapphire symbols – a blue flower, just like Millie's sapphire. "It's at the other end of the island!" she cried. "Thanks, Admiral. We know where to go now."

The albatross rolled up the map. "Take this. It'll show you if they move," he boomed. He fetched four woolly jumpers from another chest. "And you'd better

wear these again. They'll keep you dry,
like they did on your adventure with
Katie Prettywhiskers."

Goldie's jumper was yellow and Millie's
was pink. That left green and blue for the
girls.

They grinned as they put them on.
"Thanks, Admiral!"

As they left the ship, waving goodbye,
Millie scampered downhill towards the
beach.

"Wait! Won't that way be dangerous?"
called Goldie. "The waves are so huge
now the sapphire's missing!"

"It's the quickest way," Millie yelled back. "There are so many hills in the middle of the island."

They kept to the top of the beach for safety, but had to leap clear of thundering waves every so often. Their jumpers were soon wet with spray, but underneath they were dry.

After a while they passed a campsite with small, round, orange tents.

"Who's staying there?" wondered Goldie.

"Listen!" said Jess.

Anxious voices cried, "Help! Help!"

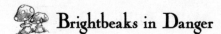

"There!" cried
Lily, looking out
over the water.
"On that huge
rock. Puffins!"

The black and white birds
were huddled with their eyes
shut tight and their bright, striped
beaks pressed together. There were
two big ones, two little ones
and a teeny tiny chick. They
clasped one another tightly
with their wings as the waves

splashed them.

Jess waved. "Hi! Over here!"

The biggest bird looked around. "We're trapped!" he squawked. "Our feathers are too drenched for us to fly!"

"We're the Brightbeak family," cried the other big one. "We're on a camping holiday, but we can't get back to our tents!"

Lily looked at Jess. "We must help them!" she said.

Jess went to the water's edge. "It's shallow enough for us to get through."

"Come on, then," said Millie.

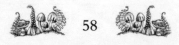

But Lily told her to wait on shore. "It's too deep for your little legs," she said.

"Okay, but I can still help," said Millie. "I'll shout when big waves come, so you don't get knocked over."

Jess hugged her. "Great!"

So Goldie and the girls splashed out to the rock, pushing through the rolling waves.

"We'll carry you back!" Lily called to the puffins.

"Oh, dear," said Mrs Brightbeak. "These waves are much bigger than us!"

Jess reached the rock they were standing

59

on. "We'll hold you tight," she promised. "And Millie will warn us about any big waves. You'll be quite safe."

Mr Brightbeak brushed a wing over his forehead with relief. "Thank you! Little ones, you go first. Pedro?"

Pedro nodded his stripy beak. Jess snuggled him into her jumper and set off.

"Roxy?" said Mrs Brightbeak.

A tiny little beak poked out from behind her. It was the adorable little puffin chick!

Lily gently picked her up and popped her in her jumper pocket. "Don't be afraid, Roxy," she said.

"WAVE!" shouted Millie.

Lily glanced over her shoulder. The wave was racing towards her. She stiffened her back, standing firm until it passed. Then she hurried to shore and set Roxy down beside Pedro. Goldie brought the third puffin chick. Millie took her jumper off and wrapped it around them.

"Thank you!" cried Pedro and Roxy,
as Millie wrapped them all up together.

Jess and Lily went back for Mr and Mrs
Brightbeak. Twice they heard, "WAVE!"
and stood stiffly until they passed. But
finally they reached the shore, and the

 62

Brightbeak family was back together!
They wrapped their wings around one
another happily.

Mrs Brightbeak hopped off towards the
campsite. She came back with a paper
bag, which she gave to Jess. "A thank-
you gift," she said, with a smile.

Inside were round, brightly coloured
sweets.

"They're Puffin Puffballs," said Pedro.
"They're like marshmallows, but even
squishier!"

Millie licked her lips. "They sound
scrummy-yummy!"

"Thanks, Mrs Brightbeak!" they said.
"We'll do our best to calm the lake,"
Goldie told the puffins.

They all waved goodbye, and the four
friends hurried on. The map told them
to turn inland, so they hurried uphill
through a copse of crab-apple trees.

Soon afterwards, Lily spotted something
red half-hidden in a bush. It was the
seahorse the imps had ridden away on!

Lily pointed it out to the others, and
Millie's eyes widened. "That means
they're close by!"

Jess grinned. "Then so is the sapphire!"

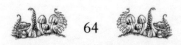

CHAPTER FIVE

Mirrors

Although the flower symbol on the map was close to where they were, it was moving around.

"The imps must be carrying it with them," said Jess. "Let's search the trees and bushes."

Millie went with Lily, and Jess went

with Goldie.

"No imps here!" Goldie called from a nutbush thicket.

"Nor here!" yelled Millie.

Lily checked the map again. "They're definitely nearby." She looked around. "But where?"

Jess spotted a huge clump of climbing dandyroses. She pulled some of the long tendrils aside to see if the imps were hiding beneath them.

She reached out, feeling around on the ground below, and touched something hard. At the same time, she heard a sound.

"There's an enormous rock under these flowers," Jess said, "and someone's singing – from inside it!"

Millie squealed and dashed over. "Is it the imps?"

They pressed their ears to the rock and heard:

"When imps be sailing the seven seas,

And the weather be wet and cold,

What warms the cockles of our hearts

Is stealing heaps of gold!"

"It's them!" said Lily.

"Let's find the way in," Goldie said.

They pulled dandyrose tendrils aside

and checked all around.

"There must be a hidden door," said Jess.

"I'll try to find it!" said Millie. She pushed her little pink snout against the rock. Then she tried a bit further along, then further still. Finally, she pushed against a flat part of the rock.

With a soft scraping sound, a little door swung open.

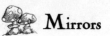

"Clever Millie!" Lily said. The little piglet's pink cheeks turned even pinker and her tiny tail curled even tighter!

Goldie and the girls had to crawl inside, but Millie was small enough to scamper in. They found themselves in a narrow tunnel, sloping downwards. Small cracks in the roof let in thin shafts of light, so they could see their way.

Soon, the tunnel widened. Here the walls were made of smooth, shiny stone. They gleamed in the light like glass.

Lily nearly yelped in fright when she saw someone standing right in front of her.

Herself!

"Wow!" she laughed. "The walls are like mirrors."

"You're right," Jess said. "I can see reflections of myself everywhere. It's like being in Millie's Hall of Funny Mirrors."

Another song started.

"*Ohhhhhh!*

If you ever be feeling jittery,

Look about for something glittery,

Steal some treasure, me pirates bold,

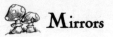

And best of all, steal heaps of gold.

Arrrrrrr!"

The four friends crept towards the sound of singing. When the tunnel widened, Jess held the others back.

"There's a cavern at the end. I think that's where the imps are!" she whispered.

Lily peered around a rocky wall, expecting to see four imps. But there were more. Far more – standing all around the cavern!

"Oh, no!" she whispered. "There are loads of them!"

But Millie bravely peered at the imps,

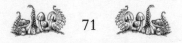

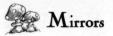

then shook her head. "It's like when we saw ourselves just now," she said. "There are only four imps – but lots of shiny reflections."

The girls and Goldie breathed big sighs of relief.

"We need to sneak in and get the sapphire," said Jess. "I'll go a bit closer."

Lily grabbed her arm. "If we can see the imps' reflections," she whispered, "they can see ours!"

She'd hardly spoken when Kelp's voice yelled, "It be them crafty girls and that cat! Come on, mateys! Run!"

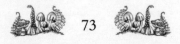

The imps disappeared at top speed down another tunnel.

"Come on!" cried Jess bravely. "After those imps!"

CHAPTER SIX
Puffin Puffballs

Jess and Lily sprinted down the tunnel after Goldie. Millie raced along behind them, her tiny trotters clacking on the stony floor.

They rounded a bend and stopped in surprise. The imps had vanished!

"Where are they?" asked Jess.

"There's one!" said Millie. "After him!"

She ran straight into a shiny wall!

"Ouch!"

"Poor Millie!" cried Lily, picking her up. "It was just a reflection!" She rubbed Millie's snout until it felt better.

"These mirrored walls make it hard to find anything," said Jess. "Oh!" She spun around. "Sorry, Lily, I was talking to your reflection!"

"If we can't tell what's real," said Goldie, "we'll never catch the imps. And if we go much deeper into these tunnels, we'll never find our way out!" Her tail twitched with worry.

Jess nodded. "I wish we had some string, so we could leave a trail to follow back."

Lily grinned and shook the paper bag Mrs Brightbeak had given them. "Puffin Puffballs!" she said. "If we leave them along the tunnels, we can follow them back to find our way out."

"Brilliant!" said Jess.

They set off. Every time they reached a turning, Lily dropped a Puffin Puffball. The bright colours of the sweets glowed in the thin cold shafts of light from the roof.

As they rounded a sharp corner, the shiny walls changed. They weren't flat any more, but had lots of curves and bumps on them.

Millie giggled. "It really is like the Hall of Funny Mirrors now!"

Despite their worries about the sapphire, the girls couldn't help laughing at Millie's reflection in the wall. It had legs like tree trunks, and trotters like tiny clothes pegs. Her floppy ears looked like sunshades, and her snout looked like a little pink button.

"Shh!" said Goldie. "I think the imps have stopped."

They peered around the next bend. The imps were sitting in a circle in the middle of a cavern. The sapphire glittered between them.

"Let's have a singsong," said Urchin, pulling what looked like seaweed sandwiches from her pocket. She munched happily as Kelp sang.

"We've got the shiny sapphire,
We're in a shiny cave.
Grizelda will be pleased with us,
Because we are so brave."

 79

The others joined in the chorus.

"*Ohhhhhh!*

Urchin, Barnacle, Kelp and Shrimp –

Who's the bravest, smartest imp?"

Then they all bellowed, "*ME!*" and fell

about laughing.

The four friends backed around the

corner, out of sight.

"How can we get the sapphire?" asked

Millie.

"I know!" said Lily suddenly. "The

imps love shiny things. We could make

them think there are lots more jewels

here. Then when they come and grab

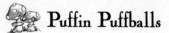

them, we can get the sapphire!"

"Great idea!" said Jess.

She piled the remaining Puffin Puffballs
into a colourful heap, just where the imps
could see them.

The shiny walls made the pile look
huge, and the reflections glittered like
dazzling gems.

Lily said loudly, "Oh, no! I've lost the
jewels we brought with us!"

Jess grinned. "How terrible! They're
the biggest and shiniest I've ever seen. I
hope Grizelda doesn't find them!"

They heard the imps leaping up.

"Jewels?" said
Shrimp. He took a
handful of gold coins
from his pocket.
"Jewels be even
better than gold!"

"That's right,
matey," said Kelp. "If there be jewels, we
be having them. Come on, me hearties!
Quietly…"

Jess pressed Lily's hand. "Now's our
chance!" she whispered. "Let's grab that
sapphire!"

CHAPTER SEVEN

Glitter Monsters

Kelp was too fast. Before either of
the girls could move, he'd reached out
with his net and snatched one of the
Puffin Puffballs.

He took it from the net and shouted
angrily, "It be sticky! It's not a jewel – it
be a dirty trick!"

 83

Lily groaned as the imps dashed back
to the sapphire. "Now what do we do?"

Millie looked at the shining walls.
"Benji and I love pulling faces in the Hall
of Funny Mirrors," she said. "It makes
us look like monsters! Maybe we could
make the imps think there are monsters
down here and scare them away?"

"That could work!" Jess said. "There's a
shiny wall that's really close to the imps.
Millie, could you use it to be a scary
monster?"

The piglet nodded bravely.

"So can I!" Lily said.

"Me, too," said Goldie.

So Lily, Goldie and Millie stood where they'd be reflected in the shiny wall, while Jess strode into the cavern.

The imps leaped up. "Shiver me timbers! Get you away!" cried Urchin.

"We not be scared of you," said Barnacle, shaking her sticky fists.

Shrimp bounced up and down, making his armbands wobble. "I be making you walk the plank!" he shouted.

"Don't be silly," said Jess. "You haven't got a plank. I came to tell you something very important."

"Oh?" sneered Kelp. "What be that?"

Jess went closer. "There are glitter monsters down here!"

The imps looked puzzled.

"What be glitter monsters?" Kelp asked suspiciously.

"They've got great big teeth and giant claws," said Jess, "and they love stealing shiny things – like gold."

The imps yelped and patted their pockets.

"No monster's stealing our gold!" Urchin shouted.

Jess grinned. "These will." She pointed to the shiny, bumpy wall.

Millie, Lily and Goldie were pulling truly horrible faces! Their teeth looked enormous, and Goldie's claws looked ferocious!

The imps shrieked in fright. "Help!"

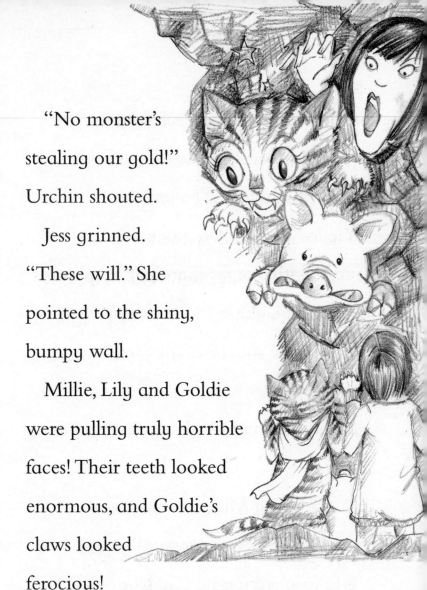

they yelled, clutching each other.

"You'll be safe this way!" Jess said, trying not to laugh. "Follow me!"

She led them down a new tunnel, and noticed with delight that they were so scared of the glitter monsters that they'd forgotten the sapphire. The plan had worked!

Millie, Lily and Goldie darted into the cavern.

"Wow!" said Millie, picking up the sapphire. "That was exciting!"

Lily scooped her up and whirled her around. "We've done it!"

 88

"Now, let's try to meet up with Jess,"
said Goldie.

They followed the trail of Puffin
Puffballs back through the tunnels and
crawled out into fresh air.

Jess was waiting for them!

Lily hugged her. "The monster trick
fooled the imps!"

Jess grinned. "They're hiding down one
of the tunnels," she said. "I expect they'll
soon realise they've been tricked."

"Let's leave the door open so they can
find the way out," said Lily. "They'll be
in enough trouble with Grizelda for losing

the sapphire. We don't want them to be stuck in the tunnels for ever!"

Goldie propped the door open with a stone, and the four friends headed for the beach. On the way they collected the red seahorse the imps had stolen. Jess and Lily carried it back between them.

Shimmer Lake was wilder than ever! When they reached the wooden pier, waves were

crashing over the funfair rides. Everything was drenched. The balloons had burst and streamers were trailing in the water like bright seaweed. The animals were huddled together, sheltering in cottage doorways.

Mr Picklesnout and Benji rushed out

to meet them.

"Has anyone seen the blue shell?" Millie yelled over the noise of the waves.

Benji held it out. "A wave washed it ashore!" he shouted.

Millie ran to him and placed the sapphire inside the shell.

Instantly the waves became smaller, until they were just gentle ripples. There were cheers from the beach as the animals came out from their shelters. They had done it! Benji and Millie spun around together in a happy dance, their little legs criss-crossing and their trotters

tapping. The girls and Goldie cheered.

"I'll never take the sapphire out, ever again," said Millie, with a relieved sigh.

Jess smiled. "Perhaps you should find a new hiding place for it," she suggested. "Maybe in the Hall of Funny Mirrors? Anyone who tried to steal the sapphire would end up very confused!"

 93

Everyone laughed. "Great idea," said Mr Picklesnout. He took the sapphire and went to hide it safely.

Millie pointed to the funfair rides. "Look, the sunshine's drying them." She grinned. "We can open the fair again!"

CHAPTER EIGHT

All the Fun of the Fair!

"Wheee!" squeaked the Twinkletail mice
in glee, spinning around on the Twirly
Teacup ride.

Jess and Lily were in one of the
Bumper Dumper Carts, giggling as
Mr Cleverfeather the owl drove straight
at them.

 95

"Gotch out, whirls!" he cried, muddling his words as usual. "I mean, watch out, girls!"

His cart drove into the side of theirs. *Thump!* He drove off, hooting with laughter.

Goldie was on the swinging boat with the Sparklepaw cats, giggling as it went higher and higher.

"Anyone want a go in the Tunnel of Laughs?" Millie called to the animals. "You'll chuckle! You'll chortle! And if you don't, we'll tickle you until you do!"

Everyone laughed. "Me! Me!" shouted

the Prickleback hedgehogs.

Lily pointed to the Water Whirl. "Let's have another ride," she said, "without Grizelda spoiling it this time!"

"We're coming too!" cried Millie, holding Benji's trotter.

As they climbed onto seahorses, a family of birds flew over. It was the Brightbeak puffins!

"I want to ride with Jess!" shouted Pedro, fluttering down.

"I want to ride with Goldie!" shouted Jade.

"Lily, take me!" cried Roxy, flapping

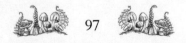

her tiny wings excitedly.

Lily tucked the little chick into her front pocket.

As the jingly-jangly music grew louder, the Water Whirl started. They rode out over the lake, around the pillar.

"Whoop! Whoop!" Roxy squawked. "This is the best holiday I've ever had!"

Benji was having such fun he couldn't stop snorting with laughter!

When the ride ended, the Brightbeaks flew off to peck some popcorn. Goldie joined Millie, Benji and the girls at the Crazy Crackers Funhouse, then the

Here-we-go Helter Skelter. Finally, they had a good laugh in the Hall of Funny Mirrors.

Before long the sun was setting and it was time to go home.

Millie and Benji hugged Goldie and the girls.

"Come and see us again soon," said Millie. "You can have a go on our rides whenever you like!"

"Thanks!" said Lily. "It was so much fun. Bye, Millie! Bye, Benji!"

"Bye, Mr

Picklesnout," added Jess. "Your funfair's brilliant!"

The Paddlefoots were waiting to sail the friends back across the lake.

"It's lovely now the water's calm again," said Jess, watching the dazzling orange and yellow sunset reflected in the lake.

Lily smiled happily. "Everything's so beautiful. We can't let Grizelda spoil it."

"If she tries," said Goldie, "I'll come and fetch you again."

When they reached shore, the girls thanked the Paddlefoots and gave Phoebe a goodbye cuddle. Then they walked through the forest to the Friendship Tree.

Goldie touched a paw to the trunk, and a little door appeared.

"Goodbye, Jess and Lily," she said. "We're so happy you helped us save Sapphire Isle and Shimmer Lake from Grizelda."

"We're happy to have so many wonderful friends!" said Lily.

They hugged.

"See you soon!" said Jess, and they stepped through the door into a shimmering golden glow.

As the light faded, the girls found

102

themselves back in Brightley Meadow. They clasped hands and ran back to Helping Paw. As always, no time had passed while they were in Friendship Forest, so no one had realised they'd gone.

"What a fantastic adventure!" said Jess.

Just then, Mrs Hart came out of the hospital. She showed them a box. "It's a pump," she said, "so we can make a fountain in the new pond!"

By the time the pond was completely filled, the fountain was in place. Mrs Hart switched it on, and water shot up high, splashing back into the pond.

The three ducklings launched themselves onto the water and quacked happily, enjoying the gentle spray. They swam around the fountain in a ring.

Mrs Hart went back indoors and the two girls sat by the pond. Lily grinned. "The ducklings look like they're having a ride on Millie's Water Whirl!"

Jess laughed. "They do! I'm so glad Friendship Forest is safe again," she said. "Let's hope Grizelda stops stealing the sapphires."

Lily nodded. "But if she tries anything, we'll be ready for her!"

The End

It's time for the Friendship Forest Swimming Gala.
But beautiful Shimmer Lake is overflowing! Can
adorable seal pup Amy Snowycoat help save
Sapphire Isle from being flooded?

Find out in the next adventure,

Amy Snowycoat's Daring Dive

Turn over for a sneak peek . . .

"Nearly finished!" Lily Hart said, shaking water from her hands.

She and her best friend, Jess Forester, were planting reeds at the edge of a pond they'd been building. It was near the Helping Paw Wildlife Hospital, which Lily's parents ran in a barn in their garden. Both girls adored animals, and loved spending their spare time helping out at the hospital.

Some of the patients were watching from nearby pens. A little fox cub sat with her head on one side, and two fluffy bunnies woffled their noses as they peeped at the girls.

"Ducks and frogs will love the pond," said Jess. "Insects, too!" She smiled as a shimmering blue dragonfly perched on a lily pad that was drifting across the pond. "It looks like it's having a ride!"

Lily grinned. "Like we did when we floated on those giant lily pads to Sapphire Isle!"

Sapphire Isle was in a secret place called Friendship Forest. The girls' friend, Goldie the cat, had taken them on lots of amazing adventures there. It was a magical world where the animals could talk! They lived in little cottages, and met their friends in the Toadstool Café to drink honey and raspberry smoothies.

"I hope we go back to Friendship Forest soon," Lily said. Then she spotted something moving in the reeds. A flash of golden fur!

Out stepped a beautiful green-eyed cat.

"Goldie!" the girls cried.

She curled around their ankles, purring. Then, with a quick glance up at the girls, Goldie darted towards Brightley Stream at the bottom of the garden.

"Come on, Lily!" said Jess. "We're going to Friendship Forest!"

They raced after Goldie, across the stream's stepping stones, into Brightley Meadow.

"Maybe Grizelda's causing trouble again," said Lily.

Read

Amy Snowycoat's Daring Dive

to find out what happens next!

Magic
Animal Friends

Can Jess and Lily save the beautiful Sapphire Isle and Shimmer Lake from Grizelda? Read all of series five to find out!

www.magicanimalfriends.com

Jess and Lily's Animal Facts

Lily and Jess love lots of different animals –
both in Friendship Forest
and in the real world.

Here are their top facts about

PIGS

like Millie Picklesnout:

- Pigs are omnivores, which means they can eat plants and animals. Newborn piglets only drink milk. Older piglets eat a mixture of corn, fruit and vegetables.

- Pigs are highly intelligent and can be trained to do tricks.

- Female pigs are called sows and can give birth to up to 25 piglets at a time.

- A group of piglets is called a 'litter'.

Can you keep the secret?

There's lots of fun for everyone at
www.magicanimalfriends.com

Play games and explore the secret world of
Friendship Forest, where animals can talk!

Join the
Magic Animal Friends Club!

→✕ Special competitions →✕

→✕ Exclusive content →✕

→✕ All the latest Magic Animal Friends news! →✕

To join the Club, simply go to

www.magicanimalfriends.com/join-our-club/